WACO-McLENNAN CO
1717 AUSTIN
WACO, TX 76

Unlocking the Secrets of Science

Profiling 20th Century Achievers in Science, Medicine, and Technology

Luis Alvarez and the Development of the Bubble Chamber

Amy Allison

Mitchell Lane
PUBLISHERS

PO Box 619 • Bear, Delaware 19701
www.mitchelllane.com

Unlocking the Secrets of Science

Profiling 20th Century Achievers in Science, Medicine, and Technology

Marc Andreessen and the Development of the Web Browser
Frederick Banting and the Discovery of Insulin
Jonas Salk and the Polio Vaccine
Wallace Carothers and the Story of DuPont Nylon
Tim Berners-Lee and the Development of the World Wide Web
Robert A. Weinberg and the Search for the Cause of Cancer
Alexander Fleming and the Story of Penicillin
Robert Goddard and the Liquid Rocket Engine
Oswald Avery and the Story of DNA
Edward Teller and the Development of the Hydrogen Bomb
Stephen Wozniak and the Story of Apple Computer
Barbara McClintock: Pioneering Geneticist
Wilhelm Roentgen and the Discovery of X Rays
Gerhard Domagk and the Discovery of Sulfa
Willem Kolff and the Invention of the Dialysis Machine
Robert Jarvik and the First Artificial Heart
Chester Carlson and the Development of Xerography
Joseph E. Murray and the Story of the First Human Kidney Transplant
Albert Einstein and the Theory of Relativity
Edward Roberts and the Story of the Personal Computer
Godfrey Hounsfield and the Invention of CAT Scans
Christiaan Barnard and the Story of the First Successful Heart Transplant
Selman Waksman and the Discovery of Streptomycin
Paul Ehrlich and Modern Drug Development
Sally Ride: The Story of the First American Female in Space
Luis Alvarez and the Development of the Bubble Chamber
Jacques-Yves Cousteau: His Story Under the Sea
Francis Crick and James Watson: Pioneers in DNA Research
Raymond Damadian and the Development of the MRI
Linus Pauling and the Chemical Bond
Willem Einthoven and the Story of Electrocardiography
Edwin Hubble and the Theory of the Expanding Universe
Henry Ford and the Assembly Line
Enrico Fermi and the Nuclear Reactor
Otto Hahn and the Story of Nuclear Fission
Charles Richter and the Story of the Richter Scale
Philo T. Farnsworth: The Life of Television's Forgotten Inventor
John R. Pierce: Pioneer in Satellite Communications

Unlocking the Secrets of Science

Profiling 20th Century Achievers in Science, Medicine, and Technology

Luis Alvarez and the Development of the Bubble Chamber

Copyright © 2003 by Mitchell Lane Publishers, Inc. All rights reserved. No part of this book may be reproduced without written permission from the publisher. Printed and bound in the United States of America.

Printing   1   2   3   4   5   6   7   8   9   10

Library of Congress Cataloging-in-Publication Data
Allison, Amy, 1956-
    Luis Alvarez and the development of the bubble chamber/Amy Allison.
       p. cm. — (Unlocking the secrets of science)
    Summary: Examines the life of the physicist who, among other achievements, was awarded the 1968 Nobel Prize for physics for developing the hydrogen bubble chamber, a powerful tool for tracking atomic particles.
    Includes bibliographical references and index.
    ISBN 1-58415-140-4 (lib. bdg.)
    1. Alvarez, Luis W., 1911—Juvenile literature. 2. Nuclear physicists—United States—Biography—Juvenile literature. 3. Bubble chambers—Juvenile literature. [1. Alvarez, Luis W., 1911- 2. Physicists. 3. Nobel Prizes—Biography. 4. Bubble chambers.] I. Title. II. Series.
QC774.A49 L68 2002
539.7'092—dc21
[B]   2002023659

ABOUT THE AUTHOR: Like Luis Alvarez, Amy Allison once called San Francisco, California home. She now lives in the Los Angeles area with her husband, Dave. Allison also wrote biographies about Antonio Banderas and John Leguizamo. Both books are part of the Latinos in the Limelight series by Chelsea House. Allison has written several other nonfiction books. *The School Library Journal* called Allison's *Shakespeare's Globe*, published by Lucent Books, "an engaging read." *Cricket* and *Jack and Jill* magazines have published Allison's poetry.

PHOTO CREDITS: cover: Photo Researchers; p. 6 Marvis; p. 9 Photo Researchers; pp. 10, 14, 18, 20, 24, 25, 26 Corbis; pp. 28, 34 Marvis; pp. 39, 40 Corbis.

PUBLISHER'S NOTE: In selecting those persons to be profiled in this series, we first attempted to identify the most notable accomplishments of the 20th century in science, medicine, and technology. When we were done, we noted a serious deficiency in the inclusion of women. For the greater part of the 20th century science, medicine, and technology were male-dominated fields. In many cases, the contributions of women went unrecognized. Women have tried for years to be included in these areas, and in many cases, women worked side by side with men who took credit for their ideas and discoveries. Even as we move forward into the 21st century, we find women still sadly underrepresented. It is not an oversight, therefore, that we profiled mostly male achievers. Information simply does not exist to include a fair selection of women.

Contents

Chapter 1
The Nobel Prize — 7

Chapter 2
Falling in Love with Physics — 11

Chapter 3
Making a Name in Physics — 15

Chapter 4
Luie's Gadgets — 21

Chapter 5
Developing the Bubble Chamber — 29

Chapter 6
Benefits of the Bubble Chamber — 35

Chapter 7
Dinosaurs and Other Discoveries — 41

Chronology — 45

Timeline — 46

Further Reading — 46

Glossary of Terms — 47

Index — 48

This portrait of Luis Alvarez was taken in 1962, before he was awarded the Nobel Prize for his development of the bubble chamber, which scientists use to track particles.

Chapter 1
The Nobel Prize

Even for a scientist, winning the Nobel Prize can seem like a fairy tale. Winners attend a glitzy ceremony, followed by a banquet in their honor. At the ceremony, a king hands them their prize. Winners of the Nobel Prize themselves enter a kind of royalty. People look up to them for reaching the height of their profession. In 1968, Luis Alvarez joined this special group.

At 4:30 p.m. on December 10, 1968, Luis stood in the wings of the Grand Auditorium of the Stockholm Concert Hall in Sweden. The Nobel ceremony honoring him as the year's physics prize winner was about to begin. In his autobiography, *Alvarez: Adventures of a Physicist*, Luis described this moment as "one of the most spine-tingling experiences of my life."

Luis listened for the blare of trumpets announcing the entrance of the Nobel winners onto the stage of the auditorium. Alfred Nobel listed physics first in his will granting the awards. So, Luis led the others in taking their places onstage. The winners followed in this order: chemistry, medicine, and literature.

King Gustaf Adolf VI of Sweden stood by his throne to hand out the prizes. The throne extended out from the stage on the auditorium floor below. After receiving his prize, Luis strode back to his place on the stage. He passed his wife, Jan. She was sitting in the auditorium's front row. They touched hands. After his own presentation, Luis could relax. He scanned the faces in the audience. When he spotted colleagues from the University of California, Berkeley he caught their eye. He nodded when they waved to him.

Under his tuxedo jacket, Luis wore a white vest. Edwin McMillan, the physics winner from U.C. Berkeley before him, passed the vest on to him. McMillan wore the vest at the Nobel ceremony honoring his win. Most Berkeley winners before McMillan wore the vest when accepting their own award. Luis was pleased to carry on the tradition.

After the ceremony, Luis and Jan were whisked into a limousine. The limousine drove them to the Stockholm City Hall for the Nobel banquet. There they joined about 1,200 guests. At 7 p.m., Luis and the other prize winners entered the banquet hall. Organ music played as they made their way down a grand staircase. They then took their seats at the 82-foot-long head table at the center of the hall.

After a dessert of ice cream, each Nobel winner gave a brief speech. In his speech, Luis acknowledged the debt he owed former physics honoree Ernest Lawrence. Lawrence started the radiation lab at U.C. Berkeley where Luis had done his prize-winning work. Luis recognized that his work built on the achievements of scientists before him. Not only did such forerunners blaze a trail, they also inspired others to follow.

"Most of us who become experimental physicists do so for two reasons," Luis wrote in his autobiography. "We love the tools of physics . . . and we dream of finding new secrets of nature as important and exciting as those our scientific heroes revealed."

Luis' scientific hero was British physicist Ernest Rutherford. Early in the 20th century, Rutherford probed

Luis' work on the bubble chamber relied on the previous discoveries of many scientists and on the hard work of many others who worked alongside him. Luis recognized these contributions when he received his Nobel Prize.

the secrets of the atom. He discovered the nucleus at the atom's core. Rutherford's discovery paved the way for more and more particles to be found in the atom. In the 1950s and 1960s, physicists identifed so many new particles that they joked about a particle zoo.

"Many particles have been discovered and studied during the last two decades," Swedish scientist Sten von Friesen said when introducing Luis at the Nobel ceremony. "They are so minute that it is impossible to see them; they can only be identified by the tracks they leave behind them as they move. The scientist must behave like the hunter, who determines the identity and behavior of his quarry by studying tracks left in the snow."

Luis won his prize for supplying particle hunters with his version of a powerful tracking tool called the bubble chamber. Equipped with this tool, scientists are coming closer to revealing nature's innermost secrets.

Luis showed a passion for science early in his education. Though he started out as a chemistry major, he hated the smells in the chemistry lab and soon discovered physics. "It was love at first sight," Luis has said. But switching his major in his junior year of college caused him to play "catch-up" with his courses. Still, he loved physics so much, he completed his coursework three months early. In this photo, he is shown in his laboratory preparing to evacuate a Geiger counter, which is used to measure radioactivity.

Chapter 2
Falling in Love with Physics

Luis was born into a family of adventurous spirits. While in his teens, his paternal grandfather sailed from Cuba to find his fortune in California. There, he found success in real estate before switching careers to medicine. Luis' father, Walter Alvarez, also worked in the medical field, building a successful practice in San Francisco, California.

On his mother's side, Luis' other grandfather also wandered far from home. He left Ireland to found a missionary school halfway around the world in China. His daughter, Harriet Smyth, left home to make a life for herself too. She attended college in Berkeley, California to train to be a teacher. Walter Alvarez was studying medicine in neighboring San Francisco when they met. The two married in 1907.

Luis was born four years later on June 13, 1911. He showed an interest in tools and gadgets early on. When Walter took Luis in 1915 to the San Francisco Panama-Pacific International Exhibition, Walter noticed his four-year-old son's fascination with exhibits in the Hall of Machinery.

Indulging America's growing enthusiasm for machines, the Hall of Machinery took up an entire 8 1/2 acres. Exhibits introduced gizmos to the public, such as drilling machines, cement mixers, electric fans, elevators, and a 500-horsepower diesel engine.

The speed and precision of such machinery boosted people's confidence in progress. America in the early 1900s was full of optimism, and optimism fueled ambitious plans. Builders were thinking big, from skyscrapers to colossal department stores. At the same time, distances were shrinking. People and ideas were on the move. Inventions, such as the automobile and the telephone, added to the push of progress. Growing up in the city, Luis felt at home in the bustling, can-do world of machinery.

In particular, the electrical equipment in his father's research lab fascinated him. As well as treating patients, Walter Alvarez pursued his interest in scientific research. On Saturdays, Luis joined his father in his lab. By age 10, Luis knew how to use every one of the lab's smaller tools. At age 11, Luis built his own radio. Homes rarely had radios in those days. They were mostly used to rescue ships. Luis himself had never heard a radio before. Still, he turned a crystal and an ice cream carton coiled with copper wire into an operating receiver. With it he managed to tune in to radio stations in the area.

Because of Luis' interest in mechanical things, his father enrolled him in San Francisco's Polytechnic High School. Luis' life underwent a big change in his junior year. He moved in 1925 with his parents, two sisters, and brother to Rochester, Minnesota. His father had accepted a full-time research job at the Mayo Clinic there. The biggest change in Luis' life was social. In San Francisco he'd never even visited the home of a friend. But in small-town Rochester, he and friends dropped in on each other. "In Rochester, I came out of my shell," he wrote in his autobiography.

The new, more social Luis got into his share of mischief. He and a friend would sneak past guards at night and climb buildings still under construction. About such pranks Luis wrote, "I'm convinced that a controlled disrespect for authority is essential to a scientist. All the good experimental physicists I have known have had an intense curiosity that no Keep Out sign could mute."

Luis' career path clearly had science in view. So, after graduating Rochester High School in 1928, Luis enrolled in the University of Chicago in Illinois.

Luis started out as a chemistry major. But he couldn't stand the smells in the chemistry labs. Also, he was frustrated with not scoring top grades. Then he discovered physics. "It was love at first sight," Luis recalled. He switched his major in his junior year.

Even on school breaks, Luis pursued his passion for physics. During one vacation at home, he conducted an experiment. He used a phonograph record, electric light, and meter stick to measure the wavelength of light in the living room. The results appeared in the 1932 issue of the journal *School Science and Mathematics*. It was his first published scientific paper.

Switching his major forced Luis to make up classes. Still, physics so captivated him that he completed his college work three months early. For his final research project, Luis built a Geiger counter. It was the first ever built in Chicago. The Geiger counter is named for its inventor, German physicist Hans Geiger. Geiger designed the device in 1912 to detect radiation levels. He later improved on his invention in 1928, with the help of Walther Müller, another German physicist. Luis judged the Geiger counters he built "the worst counters ever constructed that actually functioned." Still, he used them to make a major discovery in the field of physics.

This photo was taken outside the Science Hall at the 1933 world's fair held in Chicago, Illinois. Luis' cosmic-ray-detection equipment was recruited for the fair. During the opening days of the fair, the American Association for the Advancement of Science was scheduled to meet and Luis attended the meeting on physics.

Chapter 3
Making a Name in Physics

In the spring of 1932, Luis started graduate school at the University of Chicago. Over the summer he had constructed a Geiger counter telescope. He built this tool based on a design by German physicist Walther Bothe. Bothe had arranged two Geiger counters in a way that identified the direction of charged particles.

Over the Thanksgiving holiday, Luis stayed on at school. He was eager to attend the American Physical Society's annual meeting. That year the University of Chicago hosted the event. One of the speakers, Manuel Vallarta, proposed using a Geiger counter telescope to solve a mystery about cosmic rays. Cosmic rays traveled to earth from outer space. Luis' graduate advisor, Arthur Compton, had studied cosmic rays. He identified them as streams of electrically charged particles caught up in the earth's atmosphere. But whether they carried a positive or negative charge was still in question.

In 1930, the Italian physicist Bruno Rossi suggested a way to answer this question. He based his method on the pull of earth's magnetic field. If the field caused more cosmic rays to arrive from the west, they carried a positive charge. If more arrived from the east, they carried a negative charge. Unfortunately, Rossi's own experiments in Florence, Italy, failed to come up with a definite answer.

Vallarta claimed that his home, Mexico City, offered a better site for showing the cosmic rays' charge. Its high altitude and closeness to the equator made it a perfect spot for observing the effects of earth's magnetic field. Vallarta ended his talk with an invitation for any interested physicists to join him in Mexico City. Together they would conduct his cosmic ray experiment.

Compton convinced Luis to sign up for the experiment. Tom Johnson, a physicist at Swarthmore College in Pennsylvania, signed up too. Next to Johnson's fancy equipment, Luis' looked primitive. Johnson had mounted his counters so they swiveled effortlessly to point east or west. Luis placed his counters on a wheelbarrow. This he moved himself, every half hour, to change their direction. Still, both telescopes registered the same result. Each detected more rays from the west. This was unexpected. Most physicists supposed the rays carried a negative charge.

Back in Chicago, Luis' cosmic-ray-detection equipment was recruited for the 1933 world's fair. During the opening days of the fair, the American Association for the Advancement of Science was scheduled to meet. Luis attended the meetings on physics. To Luis, the star of the sessions was Ernest Lawrence.

Lawrence won the Nobel Prize in 1939 for the invention of the cyclotron, a kind of particle accelerator, or atom smasher. Particle accelerators speed up particles and then shoot them at an atom's nucleus. These bullet particles shatter their target into bits. Such bits, and how they behave, reveal clues to the atom's structure.

Coincidentally, Luis' older sister, Gladys, worked as a secretary for Lawrence at U.C. Berkeley. She mentioned her brother's interest in physics to Lawrence. Lawrence agreed to meet Luis at the meeting of the American Association for the Advancement of Science in Chicago. He even invited Luis to tour the fair with him. Luis recalled in his autobiography his surprise that the famous physicist seemed "a regular guy." Lawrence also invited Luis to visit him at his research lab. Luis took up the offer. Toward the end of the summer of 1934, he drove out with his parents to California. He looked forward to seeing a research lab in action.

The lab was housed in an old wooden building on the Berkeley campus. Luis was impressed that researchers had no separate office or desk space. Also, they freely borrowed each other's equipment. In fact, they often planned experiments together. This group way of doing physics excited Luis.

In the spring of 1936, Luis found himself again heading for Berkeley. This time, a job was waiting for him at the university's radiation laboratory, nicknamed the Rad Lab. Lawrence had accepted him to train as a researcher at the lab. Earlier that year, Luis received a Ph.D. in physics from the University of Chicago. He also married. He and Geraldine Smithwick started dating the year before, when she was a senior at the University of Chicago. The day after their April wedding, the couple left for Berkeley.

On his first day of work at the Rad Lab, Luis noticed a smell that became all too familiar. It was the stink of rats. The rats belonged to Lawrence's brother, John, a physician studying possible health risks from radiation produced by the cyclotron. The rats served as test subjects in the study. Dr. Lawrence determined that cyclotron operators were being exposed to dangerously high doses of radiation. He insisted on safeguards to protect the health of operators. "I certainly owe my life to John," Luis wrote in his autobiography.

Beginning in 1938, Luis added another job to that of physics researcher. He started teaching at U.C. Berkeley. He found himself learning along with the students. In his autobiography, Luis remarked, "You don't begin to understand physics well until you teach it."

Luis was discovering gaps in his own physics education. To help fill these gaps, he regularly attended weekly discussion groups Lawrence hosted. These took place Monday nights at the U.C. Berkeley physics library. There, Rad Lab workers gathered with students of physics professor

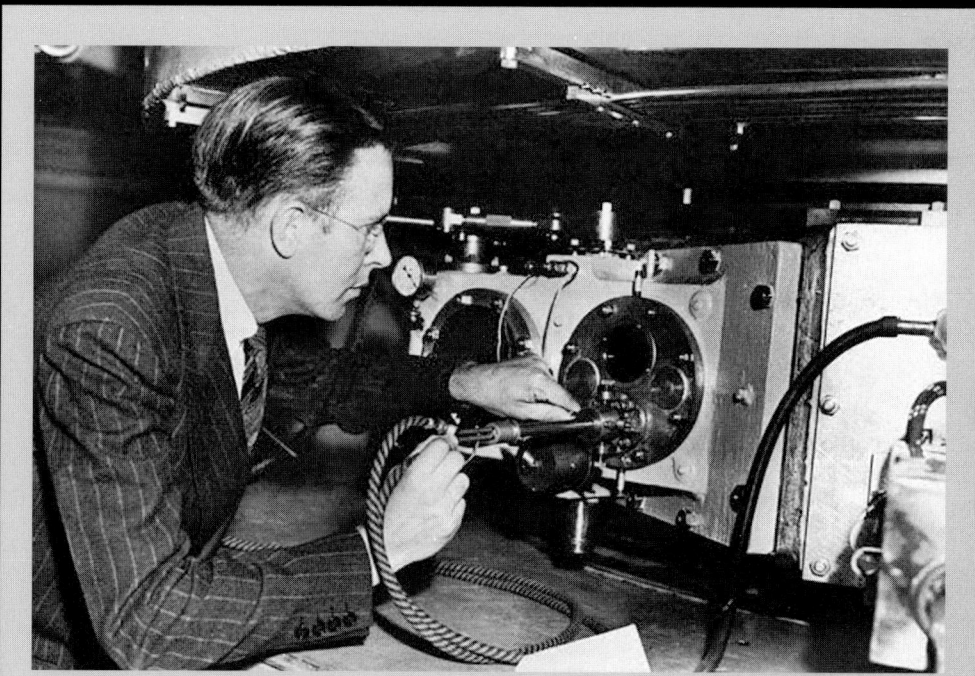

According to Luis, the star of the science sessions at the 1933 world's fair was Ernest Lawrence. Lawrence is shown here with the cyclotron he designed for producing artificial radioactivity. In 1939, he was awarded a Nobel Prize for this work.

J. Robert Oppenheimer. Researchers updated Oppenheimer and his students on experiments at the lab. They in turn updated the researchers on physics theory.

Luis benefited so much from these informal meetings that decades later he hosted them in his own home. Monday nights, Luis welcomed a crowd of 30 to 40 students into his living room. Snacks were provided, usually pretzels. No limits were placed on asking questions.

To keep up with the discussions Lawrence hosted, Luis started a nightly reading program. He was determined to read everything then written about physics. High on his reading list were three articles published in the *Reviews of Modern Physics* in 1936 and 1937. The articles surveyed in 468 pages the study of physics at the time. Physicists called the series Bethe's Bible after its main author, Hans Bethe, a physicist who later won the Nobel Prize in 1967. Reading Bethe's Bible stirred Luis' competitive spirit. Several of Luis' experiments at the Rad Lab challenged Bethe's assumptions.

The most significant experiment in Luis' career involved the two atoms, helium-3 and hydrogen-3. The 3 refers to the number of protons and neutrons in the atom's nucleus. Like Bethe, most physicists considered helium-3 radioactive and hydrogen-3 stable. That meant helium-3 was likely to break apart, while hydrogen-3 stayed in one piece. Luis proved just the opposite. He published his findings in 1940. He was beginning to make a name for himself in physics. "I suddenly surged forward from the back of the pack of young researchers," he noted in his autobiography.

J. Robert Oppenheimer was a Berkeley physics professor who suggested that unbound uranium particles might split other uranium atoms, which would start a chain reaction. Such a reaction could power factories, or destroy entire cities. Oppenheimer later became head of the Manhattan Project.

Chapter 4
Luie's Gadgets

Luis' discovery of the radioactivity of hydrogen-3 had a big impact on world affairs, as well as on his career. Hydrogen-3, or tritium, played a major role in the development of the hydrogen atom bomb. "I helped open that Pandora's box," Luis wrote in his autobiography. By this he meant he helped let the dangers of atomic warfare loose on the world. "But if I hadn't made the discovery, someone else probably would have within a year; such is the nature of most science," he added.

Before Luis published his findings on the radioactivity of tritium, startling news arrived from Germany. The news reached Luis one morning in late January 1939. He was at a barbershop, getting his hair cut. A newspaper article caught his eye. It reported that German scientists had split apart the nucleus of the uranium atom. Luis didn't wait for the barber to finish his cut. He raced off to the Rad Lab to spread the news.

The news astonished everyone. An atom's nucleus is bound together by very powerful forces. Splitting it apart would unleash a huge amount of explosive energy. Physicists refer to the shattering of the nucleus as fission. When Berkeley physics professor Oppenheimer learned that fission was now possible, he made a comment. He suggested that unbound uranium particles might split other uranium atoms. That is, a chain reaction might be started up. Such a reaction could power factories. It could also destroy cities and their populations with horrific bombs.

Bombs were not far from people's minds in 1939. World War II began that year with Nazi Germany's invasion of Poland. The following year, German bombers fired on London, England. That summer, a British scientist named Henry Tizard headed a mission to the U.S. capital. The United States had declared itself neutral in the war. Still, Tizard hoped to enlist U.S. aid in gaining on the technology front. Britain offered to share a source of microwaves its physicists developed. In turn, American physicists would use these tiny, high-powered waves to develop more accurate radar for British flyers.

The United States agreed to the deal. A secret lab opened at the Massachusetts Institute of Technology (MIT) to create the new radar system. Lawrence sat on the committee planning the project. He recruited Luis for the new MIT lab. Luis and his family had just moved into a house with a sweeping view of San Francisco Bay. The family now included a baby son, Walter. Still, Luis felt the call of duty. In November 1940, he boarded a train to Massachusetts while his family remained behind.

One of Luis' inventions at MIT helped sink plenty of Nazi submarines. It was known as VIXEN, the name for a female fox. The VIXEN system outfoxed submarine receiving devices. A British fighter plane equipped with a VIXEN system could switch its radar signals to confuse enemy submarines. So, any Nazi sub within range was misled by its own receivers. The receivers indicated the plane was flying away when it was actually approaching. The sub would then fail to duck beneath the waves for safety, and the plane could easily target the sub and fire at it.

Luis also invented a ground-controlled approach (GCA) system. This device guided a pilot to a safe landing in bad weather. In an essay entitled "The War Years," engineer Lawrence Johnston recalled the faith Luis inspired among colleagues, even when the GCA system experienced glitches.

About Luis' work style, Johnston wrote: "Luie had the faith and the imagination to build a blind landing system complete in every detail when the most essential component, the antenna . . . had only been tested in rudimentary form and those tests showed that it had serious problems. He clearly inspired faith in us who worked with him and in the administrators above him."

Administrators at the MIT lab had so much faith in Luis that they gave him his own division. That division, Special Systems, was known as Luie's Gadgets. It worked solely on Luis' designs.

By the time Luis left MIT, the United States had officially entered WWII. The government declared war in 1941 after Japanese flyers attacked U.S. ships in Pearl Harbor, Hawaii. Two years later, in 1943 Luis signed up for the Manhattan Project. The Manhattan Project was the code name for America's program to develop nuclear weapons. Luis planned to transfer to Los Alamos, New Mexico, where Oppenheimer headed the secret project to build the atom bomb.

But first Oppenheimer recommended Luis go to the Metallurgical Laboratory at the University of Chicago. There, he helped Enrico Fermi create the world's first nuclear reactor. The reactor served as a factory for producing plutonium. Plutonium created fission more readily than uranium. It was therefore seen as promising material for nuclear weapons.

Luis felt thrilled to be working with the world-famous Fermi. But he found operating the reactor more boring than operating the cyclotron back at the Rad Lab. He looked forward to leaving for Los Alamos after his six-month assignment in Chicago.

Luis arrived in Los Alamos in 1944. Soon after, Luis' family, which now included baby daughter Jean, joined him. Housing officers for the project assigned the Alvarezes a barracks-style apartment house with tin showers and wood-burning stoves. Neighbors protested when they found out a Hispanic family was moving in. In those days, Americans

Enrico Fermi is pictured here inspecting equipment at the laboratory at Columbia University in 1939. Fermi was the famed Italian physicist who won the 1938 Nobel Prize for his discovery of radioactive substances. Alvarez helped Fermi create the world's first nuclear reactor at the University of Chicago in the 1940s.

Tourists at the Alamogordo, New Mexico site look at a bomb casing like that of "Fat Man," one of the first atomic bombs.

didn't bother to hide their prejudice against minorities. Fortunately, a friend of the Alvarezes ran the housing office. Nothing came of the protests.

Luis found working on the Manhattan Project exciting. He led a team to develop a detonator, or trigger, for a plutonium bomb called Fat Man. The quickness of plutonium to fission threatened to fizzle Fat Man's explosion. Its detonation needed to be more controlled than that of a uranium bomb called Little Boy, which had a point-blank, gun-like trigger. Luis' team produced a kind of explosive shell surrounding the plutonium. The shell featured evenly spaced detonation points. These produced a shock wave when fired at the same time. The wave squeezed the plutonium to the point of making fission without jeopardizing the force of Fat Man's explosion.

In April 1945, Luis took on a new assignment. Oppenheimer asked him to come up with a way to measure the explosive energy of atomic bombs that would fire on Japan. Luis designed a microphone whose signal would increase as the bomb's blast wave hit it and decrease as the wave passed it by. A set of these microphone gauges hung from a parachute. The parachute dropped from a plane following behind the B-29 bomber loaded with Little Boy.

Luis planned a practice run with members of his team on July 16, 1945. On that day, the world's first atom bomb was tested at Alamogordo, New Mexico. But on July 15, Luis and his team got new orders. They were forbidden to fly any closer than 25 miles from the test site. That meant their detector wouldn't pass an important test before the actual bombing mission.

The mission was less than a month away. Later in July, Luis flew to the U.S. air base on Tinian, an island in the Pacific Ocean. A couple of members from his team joined

The first atomic bomb explodes at Alamogordo, New Mexico on July 16, 1945.

him. They planned to operate the equipment measuring the force of the uranium bomb. All the men flying the mission were told to make out a will. There was real danger they wouldn't make it home alive. Luis and each of his colleagues were issued a combat flying suit. It came equipped with a parachute, inflatable life raft, and first-aid kit. Over this went a flack suit to protect the body from flying bombshell fragments.

Stormy weather held off the mission until August 6, the day before the B-29 bomber operators learned their target would be Hiroshima, Japan. Sometime before 2:45 a.m., Luis and his crew boarded their plane, the *Great Artiste*. They were too busy to be excited. By 6 a.m., they were preparing their microphone gauges for the parachute drop. They listened closely for the bomb's-away signal from the bomber loaded with Little Boy. The end of the signal was their cue to release the parachute. Little Boy hit with a force of 15,000 tons of explosives. A sudden bright flash lit the windows of the *Great Artiste*. Seconds later, two jolts shook the plane.

On the return trip to Tinian, Luis wrote a letter to his four-year-old son, Walt. In it, Luis explained his part in the fateful bombing. "What regrets I have about being party to killing and maiming thousands of Japanese civilians this morning are tempered with the hope that this terrible weapon we have created may bring the countries of the world together and prevent further wars," he wrote.

Three days later, Big Man exploded over Nagasaki, Japan. Within a week, the Japanese agreed to surrender. The threat of nuclear weapons has hung over the world ever since.

Luis Alvarez is shown with his bubble chamber display built in Berkeley, California.

Chapter 5
Developing the Bubble Chamber

Before WWII ended, Luis already was planning a project to work on back home in Berkeley. He expected to return to teaching at the university. But he also needed to be building or inventing something. At Los Alamos, he started designing a linear accelerator, or linac.

Luis planned his linac to be a more powerful atom smasher than the cyclotron. The cyclotron sped up its particle bullets in a series of circular paths. Particles in a linear accelerator instead picked up speed, and energy, along a straight path. *Linear* means straight. To speed particles to very high energies, Luis' linac would be 40 feet long. The higher the energies of the particles, the more evidence they produced when shot at their target.

Soon after returning to Berkeley, Luis assembled a team at the Rad Lab to build his linac. Construction began in 1946. A year later, the linac was up and running. Using the linac, researchers at the Rad Lab discovered several new isotopes, or atoms with different numbers of neutrons. These included nitrogen-12 and boron-8. Boron-8 would play a part in the study of particles jetting out from the sun.

The mighty linac also worked in tandem with other devices for studying particles. In 1954, the lab debuted its proton synchroton. The synchroton generated billions of volts of energy. These enormous energies were needed to create such exotic stuff as antiparticles for study. Antiparticles were twins of existing particles but with opposite charges. The Berkeley synchroton, known as the Bevatron, became the second proton synchroton ever built. The Brookhaven National Laboratory in New York built the first one two years earlier.

The linac produced an intense pulse of protons. This made it ideal for shooting proton bullets into the Bevatron's main accelerator ring. There a series of magnetic fields whipped the protons into even greater speeds before hurling them toward their target.

The Bevatron lived up to its promise. Just a year after its completion, a Berkeley team used it to produce the antiproton. The synchroton also was producing so-called strange particles. These particles lasted millions of times longer than expected. The problem was physicists lacked tools powerful enough to investigate such oddities.

The only detecting tool then available was the cloud chamber. Charles Wilson invented the cloud chamber in 1912 and shared the Nobel Prize in physics in 1927 for the invention. The clouds he saw billowing over the highlands in his native Scotland inspired Wilson. So, he tried to form clouds in a pint-size glass jar in his lab.

First, he filled the jar with moist air. Then he reduced the pressure in the jar suddenly. This cooled the air inside to the point that water vapor condensed in the jar. The vapor condensed around electrically charged particles in the air. The condensation appeared as tiny drops. Trails of drops showed a particle's path. However, these ghostly trails failed to last long enough to be studied in any detail.

In April 1953, mulling over this problem, Luis attended sessions of the American Physical Society in Washington,

D.C. On the first day, he struck up a conversation with a young physicist from the University of Michigan. The man introduced himself as Donald Glaser. Glaser confided his fear that no one would be around to hear his presentation. It was scheduled for the last session on the last day. By then, most of the attendants would be gone. Luis himself wasn't planning to stick around until the closing session. So, he offered to listen to a summary of Glaser's presentation.

Glaser explained that he had invented a new particle detector. He called it a bubble chamber. He showed Luis photos of bubble tracks captured in his chamber. Glaser's bubble chamber consisted of a thimble-size glass bulb. The bulb contained ether in liquid form. Superheating the ether revealed the presence of charged particles. Superheating involved suddenly reducing the pressure below the level where a liquid boils. When superheated, the ether boiled only where the charged particles passed. This left behind a track of bubbles.

Luis quickly recognized the value of Glaser's invention. Liquid was denser than the water vapor that filled cloud chambers. It therefore offered a longer look at particles under investigation. Scientists could then delve deeper into the evidence.

That night Luis discussed building a bigger, better bubble chamber with a couple of Berkeley colleagues. Enlarging the chamber would increase the amount of evidence it produced. Luis also suggested replacing ether with liquid hydrogen inside the chamber. The hydrogen atom is the simplest of all atoms. Filling the chamber with more complicated material only complicated the evidence. Keeping the material simple made interpretation of the evidence easier.

Back at the Rad Lab, Luis began working toward his goal. He directed the building of ever-bigger liquid hydrogen bubble chambers. A 1.5-inch test model first showed tracks in February 1954. Afterward came a 2.5-inch, a 4-inch, and then a 10-inch chamber. The 2.5-inch bubble chamber that lab technician A. J. "Pete" Schwemin built featured a major change from the 1.5-inch model. The earlier model was made entirely of glass. The 2.5-inch chamber had glass only in its viewing windows. These were bolted onto a metal-bodied chamber.

The sturdiness of metal enabled the building of bigger bubble chambers. Scientists had avoided metal until Schwemin's model. Unlike smooth glass, metal produced rough spots where accidental boiling could occur. In the 2.5-inch chamber, bubbles at chamber walls posed no problem after all. Superheating didn't break down throughout the chamber as feared. As long as it was large enough, a bubble chamber could sustain superheating without being all glass. Based on the success of his test models, Luis made a bold proposal. In April 1955, he suggested building a 72-inch bubble chamber. A chamber this size would advance particle hunting to a new level.

"With great foresight [Luis] visualized the whole concept of large-scale bubble-chamber physics," Edwin McMillan, a colleague at Berkeley, told *Science* magazine.

Luis saw his bubble chamber as an entire research system. A flood of data was expected from a 72-inch chamber. Handling the data in an orderly, mechanized way would allow researchers to keep up with the data flow. Making the system work called for new technology. Specifically, the tasks of recording and measuring bubble chamber tracks would need to be automated. Luis drew on his wartime experience with automatic radar tracking to come up with a plan to record tracks automatically. A computer then read this record and helped analyze the data.

Photos taken by bubble chamber cameras showed particle tracks as mysterious splash patterns of lines, curves, and spirals. A computer could be programmed to translate these patterns into mathematical language that scientists understand. It could produce printouts of charts and graphs meaningful to physics researchers. Researchers could then scan the printouts for significant clues. For example, a particle's mass, or the amount of matter it contained, could be determined from bubble chamber computer data.

Luis' new bubble chamber cost about $2.5 million to build. Luis asked Lawrence for help in approaching the government for funding, despite Lawrence's skepticism of the project. "I don't believe in your big chamber," Luis recalled in a lecture following his Nobel Prize win. "But I do believe in you, and I'll help you obtain the money." The government did award Luis the money, and work on the big bubble chamber project began. Luis now had new worries.

Seven Nobel laureates posed in front of Ernest Lawrence's 37-inch cyclotron magnet. (L to R) Owen Chamberlain, Edwin McMillan, Emilio Serge, Melvin Calvin, Donald Glaser, Luis Alvarez, and Glenn Seaborg, March 7, 1969.

Chapter 6
Benefits of the Bubble Chamber

Liquid hydrogen has a dangerous tendency to explode. Even more frightening, no one had ever worked with the large amounts needed to fill Luis' 72-inch bubble chamber. So, workers on the project faced risks to their safety. Fortunately, no accidents with the element occurred during construction of the big chamber.

Luis guided the project every step of the way. Engineering student Stanley Wojcicki described Luis' bold leadership in an essay called "My First Days in the Alvarez Group."

"Luie loved new challenges and had that particular disdain of bureaucracy that characterizes many scientists," Wojcicki wrote. "For example, the 72-inch bubble chamber was built and operational before the building to house it was ready. When I asked Luie about this, he said something to the effect of, 'It's not surprising. Nobody ever built a big hydrogen bubble chamber before, so there are no rules to follow. But people have built buildings for centuries, so there are hundreds of volumes of regulations that have to be satisfied.'"

The scale of the project called for large crews of physicists, engineers, and technicians. Luis coordinated their tasks in one big organization known as the Alvarez group. Regardless of how big the organization became, Luis maintained a personal feel among the staff. Wojcicki appreciated Luis' informality.

"We all sat around a table in Luie's office and for refreshments had home-baked cookies brought by Janet Landis, the future Mrs. Alvarez, who then worked as a data analyst," Wojcicki fondly recalled about the first meeting he attended regarding the bubble chamber.

Luis married Janet Landis on December 28, 1958. Later, they had two children, Don and Helen. Luis and his first wife, Geraldine, divorced a year earlier. Luis thought he and Gerry grew apart because they'd lost the habit of sharing each other's lives. He suspected that the strict secrecy he'd worked under during WWII created this distance between them. By contrast, Jan's familiarity with Luis' work at the Rad Lab facilitated their relationship. He and Jan celebrated together when his 72-inch bubble chamber operated for the first time on March 24, 1959.

Luis shared his powerful new research tool with other physicists. He offered other physics labs the project's engineering studies. Bound together, these studies took up a whole six feet of bookshelf space. Luis hoped the labs would use the information to build bubble chambers of their own.

Luis' bubble chamber certainly contributed to the number of particles now known. His research played a part in the discovery of more than 70 elementary, or basic particles. For example, one of these particles is Y-star 1385. It has an extremely short lifetime. Moving at the speed of light, it can just cross an average-size nucleus before breaking apart.

Discovering new particles and how they behave helps scientists better understand matter in its most basic form.

Particularly, scientists hope to unlock the secrets at the heart of the atom. These secrets lie in its nucleus where powerful forces bind the nucleus together. Many believe these forces can be trusted for peaceful purposes, and not just used in weapons systems.

Nuclear energy promises to light cities and power industries. A better understanding of nuclear particles can also help ensure the safety of nuclear energy production. Accidents at nuclear power plants can be deadly. So can the radioactive waste materials produced by these plants. Safety and waste-disposal policies based on the most up-to-date nuclear research can save lives.

Nuclear medicine also hopes to save lives. Already radioactive tracers help evaluate the effectiveness of drugs on parts of the body. In addition, improvements in radiation therapy may help increase cancer survival rates.

The survival of individuals, as well as humankind, may depend on progress in nuclear research. Scientists' understanding of the basic stuff of matter helps extend our reach farther than our own planet. Matter makes up everything in the universe. Nuclear theory can help us, and generations after us, benefit from resources outside the earth. It can even lead to knowledge of how the universe began, and how it may end. Armed with this knowledge we have a better chance of controlling our destiny.

More immediate uses for the bubble chamber have been suggested by research at the Los Alamos National Laboratory in New Mexico. These uses are based on the chamber's ability to detect extremely small particles. Such particles can show as impurities in fluids down to the parts-per-trillion level. One possible application is monitoring environmental pollution. Another is assuring drug quality.

Many advances in physics research at the Los Alamos lab and elsewhere are due to Luis' development of the bubble chamber. Still, Luis' achievement did not attract widespread recognition right away. Finally, at 3:30 a.m. of October 30, 1968, that recognition came. CBS News called to tell Luis he had won the Nobel Prize.

Luis' name alone appeared on the telegram from the Nobel committee announcing his win. Still, Luis realized he hadn't built the world's top particle-tracking tool on his own. So, he spent part of his award money on plane tickets to Stockholm, Sweden for six senior members of the Alvarez group and their wives. Luis insisted they attend the Nobel ceremony with Jan and him.

At the ceremony, Professor Sten von Friesen of Sweden's Royal Academy of Sciences introduced Luis to the crowd by saying, "Practically all the discoveries that have been made in this important field of high-energy physics have been possible only through use of methods originated by Professor Alvarez." Then, he spoke directly to Luis.

"Dr. Alvarez, your contributions to physics are numerous and important," Friesen said. "Today our attention is focused on the outstanding discoveries which you have made in the field of high-energy physics, as a result of your farsighted and bold development of the hydrogen bubble-chamber into an instrument of great power and high precision, and of the means of handling and analyzing the large quantities of valuable information it can produce."

The 1968 Nobel Prize recipients: (L to R) H. Gobind Khorana, Robert W. Holley, Luis Alvarez, Marshall W. Nirenberg, Lars Onsager, and Japanese author Yasunari Kawabata.

Along with the Nobel, Luis' many honors include the Pioneer Award in 1963 from the American Institute of Electrical and Electronics Engineers, and the National Medal of Science in 1964. Also, in 1981 Luis won the Dudley Wright Prize for Interdisciplinary Science. Because of Luis' wide-ranging interests, colleagues at the Rad Lab dubbed him the prize wild-idea man. His varied interests led Luis to make significant contributions outside physics research as well.

Luis Alvarez (left) and son Walter view a sample of an iridium layer deposit, which is found worldwide. Based on this layer, the Alvarezes postulated that a giant asteroid hit the earth in the Cretaceous period, nearly 65 million years ago. With a force equal to 100 million atom bombs, the impact blasted an enormous crater in the earth. Then, a thick cloud of dust rose from the crater, blocking sunlight. It also showered down poisonous acid rain. All this triggered mass extinction of the dinosaurs, among other life forms. The Alvarezes impact theory made the cover of Time magazine and stirred up much controversy.

Chapter 7
Dinosaurs and Other Discoveries

Luis' risk-taking spirit eventually plunged him into the rough-and-tumble world of business. He launched a company with Schwemin called Schwem Technology. Schwem produced a jitter-free zoom lens for shoulder-held video cameras. Known as the Gyrozoom, it also could be mounted on TV news trucks. The Gyrozoom and other Schwem products stemmed from Luis' ideas. Luis held a total of 40 patents for his inventions. In 1978, he won election to the National Inventors Hall of Fame.

"Alvarez's whole approach in physics was that of an entrepreneur, taking big risks by building large new projects in the hope of large rewards," Berkeley colleague Richard Muller told *The New York Times*.

Luis' inventiveness spilled into an archaeological venture as well. In 1965, he and Egyptian physicist Fathy El Bedewi cofounded the Joint Pyramid Project of the United Arab Republic and the United States of America. Egyptian pharaohs built pyramids to serve as tombs. Secret, treasure-filled rooms had been found in two of three great pyramids. None, however, turned up in the third.

Luis came up with the idea to X-ray this pyramid that served as the tomb of the pharaoh Chephren. Powerful X-rays could reveal any rooms hidden in Chephren's pyramid. Luis convinced the National Geographic Society to help fund the project. The search began in earnest in June 1967. By the following February, evidence showed a spacious room under the pyramid's eastern face.

"I began dreaming of the golden artifacts we would see as we looked into Chephren's tomb, intact 4,500 years, for the first time," Luis recalled in his autobiography.

Such dreams faded after a closer look at the evidence. A programming error produced the misleading data. So, Chephren's pyramid hid no treasure chambers after all. But Luis didn't feel he'd wasted time looking.

"It wasn't that we didn't find a chamber," he wrote in his autobiography. "We found that there wasn't any chamber." Elsewhere in *Alvarez: Adventures of a Physicist*, Luis reflected, "Much of a physicist's life, both in and out of his laboratory, is spent in scientific detective work."

In the 1970s, Luis took up detective work in the field of geology. Luis' son Walter was a geologist himself. Father and son worked as a team on a case in 1976. The investigation began when Walter showed Luis a rock from Gubbio, Italy. The rock had once been on the sea floor. It consisted of two layers of limestone separated by a half-inch layer of clay.

The limestone came from seashells. The arrangement of the layers suggested the seashells had stopped settling on the sea floor for a while, then started appearing again. Apparently, tiny creatures living in the shells had dropped off in large numbers when the clay layer formed about 65 million years ago.

Walter explained the clay layer marked the boundary between the Cretaceous and Tertiary periods of geologic time. This period was known, for short, as the KT boundary. At the end of the Cretaceous period, many forms of life on earth, including the dinosaurs, died out. No one knew how.

Luis' investigation into the clay layer resulted in a surprising discovery. The KT boundary showed large amounts of an element called iridium. In fact, it contained 300 times as much iridium as the limestone layers. But iridium is rare on earth. Instead, it is most common in meteorite dust. Meteorites are objects that fall to earth from outer space.

These facts led the Alvarezes to make the following conclusion. The iridium came from an asteroid or comet estimated to be the size of San Francisco. Nearly 65 million years ago, this giant object slammed into the earth. It hit with a force equal to 100 million atom bombs. The impact blasted an enormous crater in the earth. Then, a thick cloud of dust rose from the blasted-out crater. The cloud blocked off sunlight, killing plants. It also showered down poisonous acid rain. The catastrophe triggered the mass extinction seen in the KT boundary.

The Alvarezes' impact theory made the cover of *Time* magazine and stirred up a whirlwind of controversy. Among the theory's toughest critics were paleontologists who study life from past geologic periods, such as dinosaurs. Most paleontologists dismissed the idea the dinosaurs came to a sudden, dramatic end. The media played up the conflict. Conflict sold magazines and newspapers, and raised TV news ratings.

"I don't like to say bad things about paleontologists," Luis shot back, according to *The New York Times*, "but they're not very good scientists. They're more like stamp collectors."

Probably the most damaging charge against the Alvarezes' impact theory was the absence of an impact site.

No crater then known was large enough to support the theory. Then came the discovery of the huge, 190-mile-wide Chicxulub crater in 1992. Geologists found it buried on the north coast of Mexico's Yucatán peninsula. Unfortunately, Luis never lived to see the Chicxulub crater. He died from cancer in 1988 in his Berkeley home. News of Luis' death appeared on the front page of *The New York Times*. In the article, Muller described how Luis thrived on challenges.

"Alvarez seemed to care less about the way the picture in the puzzle would look, when everything fit together, than about the fun of looking for pieces that fit," Muller said. "He loved nothing more than doing something that everyone else thought impossible."

Luis' readiness to take big risks in hopes of big rewards paid off well for science. Back to the ancient Greeks, people have wondered how nature works. Now, in the 21st century, scientists continue on the trail of nature's most basic building blocks. One of the particles they're hunting has even been called the God particle. Chances are, this mysterious particle will be spotted first in a bubble chamber, thanks to Luis.

Luis Alvarez Chronology

1911 born June 13 in San Francisco, California.

1926 moves with his family to Rochester, Minnesota.

1928 enrolls in the University of Chicago in Illinois.

1932 publishes his first scientific paper.

1933 codiscovers the East-West effect in cosmic rays.

1936 marries Geraldine Smithwick; receives Ph.D. in physics from the University of Chicago and begins work as a research associate at the University of California, Berkeley.

1940 discovers the radioactivity of tritium.

1940–43 designs radar systems at the Massachusetts Institute of Technology to aid the British in fighting World War II.

1944 joins the Manhattan Project in Los Alamos, New Mexico to help develop the atomic bomb.

1945 serves as science observer for the Hiroshima explosion; returns to U.C. Berkeley after the war ends.

1947 sees completion of his design for the 40-foot proton linear accelerator.

1955 proposes development of a 72-inch bubble chamber.

1957 divorces Geraldine.

1958 marries Janet Landis.

1964 awarded the National Medal of Science for his contributions to high-energy physics.

1965 launches project to beam cosmic rays at Egypt's Chephren pyramid to search for hidden rooms.

1968 wins the Nobel Prize in physics.

1978 named to the National Inventors Hall of Fame.

1980 announces the impact theory of mass extinctions, developed with son Walter.

1988 dies of cancer.

Bubble Chamber Timeline

1912 Charles Wilson invents the cloud chamber to track the paths of atomic particles.

1932 Carl Anderson sees evidence of an antiparticle in a cloud chamber.

1947 G. D. Rochester and C. C. Butler find strange particles in a cloud chamber.

1952 Donald Glaser invents the bubble chamber, a more sensitive particle-tracking tool than the cloud chamber.

1954 A 1.5-inch bubble chamber filled with liquid hydrogen, proposed by Luis Alvarez, shows tracks for the first time; 2.5-inch, 4-inch, and 10-inch chambers follow later that year.

1955 Luis Alvarez announces his intention to expand his hydrogen bubble chamber to 72 inches for more detailed study of strange and other exotic particles.

1958 The Alvarez group's 15-inch bubble chamber begins operation.

1959 Luis' 72-inch bubble chamber becomes a working research tool.

1960 The Alvarez group discovers a new particle, Y-star 1385, in the 72-inch chamber.

1968 The Alvarez group is analyzing more than one million bubble chamber tracks a year; Alvarez wins the Nobel Prize in physics for his "development of the hydrogen bubble chamber into an instrument of great power and high precision."

1997 A technique for using bubble chambers in the detection of impurities in fluids is announced; applications include environmental monitoring and assuring drug quality.

Further Reading

Books

Gallant, Roy. *The Ever-Changing Atom.* New York: Benchmark Books/Marshall Cavendish, 2000.

Gonzales, Doreen. *The Manhattan Project and the Atomic Bomb in American History.* Berkeley Heights, N.J.: Enslow, 2000.

Norris, Richard. *Meteorite! The Last Days of the Dinosaurs.* Austin, Tex.: Raintree Steck-Vaughn, 2000.

Olesky, Walter. *Hispanic American Scientists.* New York: Facts on File, 1998.

Web Sites

Memorial Tribute – Luis Alvarez
http://www.fas.org/rlg/alvarez.htm
Nobel Laureates – Luis Alvarez 1988 Nobel Prize for Physics
http://www-library.lbl.gov/teid/tmLib/nobellaureates/LibL_Alvarez.htm

Glossary of Terms

Atom: a bit of matter once thought to be the smallest particle; in fact, it consists of a nucleus orbited by electrons.
Charged particle: a particle with either a negative force (or charge) or a positive force (or charge); known specifically as an electrically charged particle.
Fission: the splitting of an atom's nucleus; it results in a huge release of energy.
Hydrogen: the simplest atom; it has only a single electron.
Magnetic field: an area where electric charges have an influence; equal to an electric field.
Mass extinction: the death of whole groups of plants and animals.
Matter: anything that takes up space.
Neutron: the particle partnered in the nucleus with the proton; it carries no charge.
Nuclear: having to do with the nucleus of the atom; refers to weapons whose destructive power comes from splitting the nucleus.
Nucleus: the core of the atom; the protons it contains give it a positive charge.
Physics: the study of matter and energy, and how they act on each other.
Proton: the part of the atom that carries a positive charge; this charge balances the negative charge of the atom's orbiting electrons.
Radiation: rays, or streams, of particles and energy some atoms release.
Superheated: heating a liquid just below its boiling point; this causes tiny gas bubbles to form wherever a charged particle passes.
X ray: a very high-energy type of radiation.

Index

Alvarez (Smithwick), Geraldine 17, 36
Alvarez (Smyth), Harriet 11
Alvarez (Landis), Jan 7, 8, 36
Alvarez, Luis
    awards, 7–9, 38, 39
    birth, 11
    childhood, 11–12
    children, 22, 24, 36
    death, 44
    discoveries, 15–16, 19, 21
    education, 12, 13, 15–17
    inventions
        optics, 41
        radar, 22–23
        weapons systems, 25–27
    marriages, 17, 36
    teaching career, 18
    teen years, 12–13
Alvarez, Walter (father) 11, 12
Alvarez, Walter (son) 22, 40, 42–43
Alvarezes' impact theory 42–44
Bethe, Hans 19
Bothe, Walther 19
Bubble chamber
    display of, 28
    invention of, 31
    development of, 31–33, 35–36
    importance of, 36–38
Chephren's pyramid 41–42
Compton, Arthur 15
El Bedewi, Fathy, 41
Fat Man (plutonium bomb) 25, 27
Fermi, Enrico 23, 24
Friesen, Sten von 9, 38
Geiger, Hans 13
Geiger counter 10, 13
Geiger counter telescope 15–16
Glaser, Donald 31, 34
Gyrozoom 41
Johnson, Tom 16
Lawrence, Ernest 8, 16–17, 18, 34
Little Man (uranium bomb) 25, 26, 27
Manhattan Project 23, 25
McMillan, Edwin 8, 32, 34
Muller, Richard 41, 44
Müller, Walther 13
Nobel Prize 7–9, 38, 39
Oppenheimer, J. Robert 19, 20, 21, 23, 26
Rossi, Bruno 15
Rutherford, Ernest 8–9
San Francisco Panama-Pacific International Exhibition 11
Schwemin, A. J. "Pete" 32, 41
Schwem Technology 41
Tizard, Henry 22
Vallarta, Manuel 15–16
Wilson, Charles 30
Wojcicki, Stanley 35–36
World's fair (Chicago, 1933) 14–16
World War II 21–27